D0580074

OLD MISERY

For Lewis and Louise Cullman, lovers of life — J.S.
For findacure.org.uk — R.A.

Kids Can Press gratefully acknowledges the financial support of the Government of Ontario, through the Ontario Media Development Corporation.

Published in Canada and the U.S. by Kids Can Press Ltd.
25 Dockside Drive, Toronto, ON M5A 0B5

Kids Can Press is a Corus Entertainment Inc. company

www.kidscanpress.com

The artwork in this book was rendered in pencil and digitally.
The text is set in Buccaneer.

Edited by Yasemin Uçar
Designed by Michael Reis

Printed and bound in Shenzhen, China, in 10/2017 by C&C Offset

CM 18 0 9 8 7 6 5 4 3 2 1

Library and Archives Canada Cataloguing in Publication

Sage, James, author
Old Misery / written by James Sage ; illustrated by Russell Ayto.

ISBN 978-1-77138-823-8 (hardcover)

I. Ayto, Russell, illustrator II. Title.

PZ7.S234O43 2018 j813'.54 C2017-903216-X

OLD MISERY

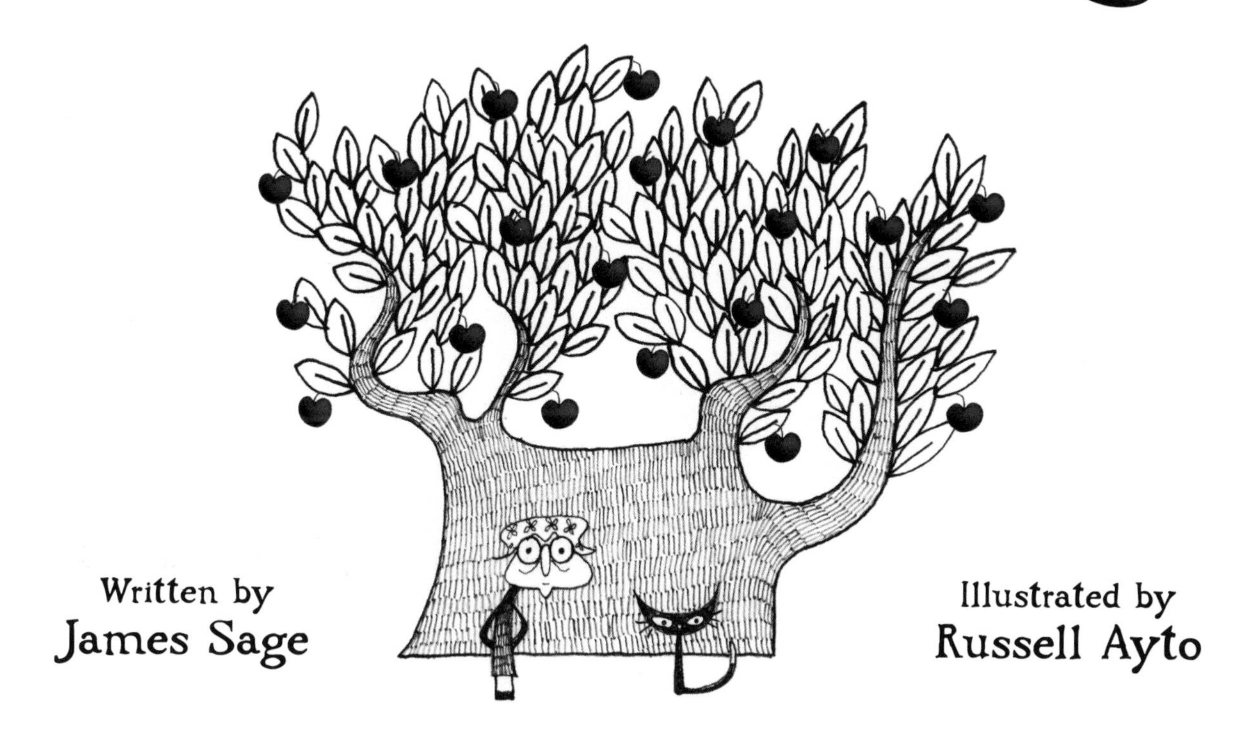

Written by
James Sage

Illustrated by
Russell Ayto

Kids Can Press

Old Misery's the name, and for good reason, too. Ain't got two pennies to rub together. Ain't got nothing except old Rutterkin here, and she's about as worthless as a dog with fleas.

MEOW-OW, MEOW-OW!

Oh, and that apple tree over yonder is mine. Good eating apples and all, *if* it wern't *for* the wicked stealing.

Out! Out! Wait 'til I catch you!

Trouble is, I can't get around as I used to. Lose my puff going uphill. Which brings to mind that fella who came by the other day – and me in my stocking feet!

Oh, he was a nice cup of tea, he was, wondering if I had any extra food lying about – as if I did!

“Well now,” says I to him, “I'm about to rustle up some potato pie *for* dinner, that's *if* I ever get started. You're welcome to share a bite with me, such as it is.”

He soon polished *off* the pie, he did, and the last *of* me rhubarb wine, too!

"My word, that was tasty!" says he. "Make yourself a wish on me, Granny, anything at all."

Now, not being one to put off 'til tomorrow what I can do today, I says to him, "There's but one wish for me, mister, and it's this here: whoever I catch stealing apples off my tree will get stuck to it until I decide to let them go!"

"Agreed, agreed!" says he.

Next day, me and Rutterkin go out to pay the apple tree a visit and this here's what we found stuck fast:

two goats,
a rooster,
one cow,
a sow with litter,
a fine lady in a yellow dress
and the local vicar looking
mighty wiffy-waffy.

Oh, I gave them some tongue, I did! Then, after a spell, but not before, I let them come down.

Why, you never saw such anshum-scranshum!

Word of this must've got round pretty quick, because the next time me and Rutterkin went visiting the tree, it was ragged with apples, enough even to put some by for winter.

"Who speaks?" says I, real polite.

"Why, they call me Mr. Death. I expect you've heard of me. Most folk have."

"Daisy me!" says I. "So it's Mr. D. come at last, is it? Well, I'm ready to go with you anytime, only maybe you'd oblige me with one last little *fancy* ...?"

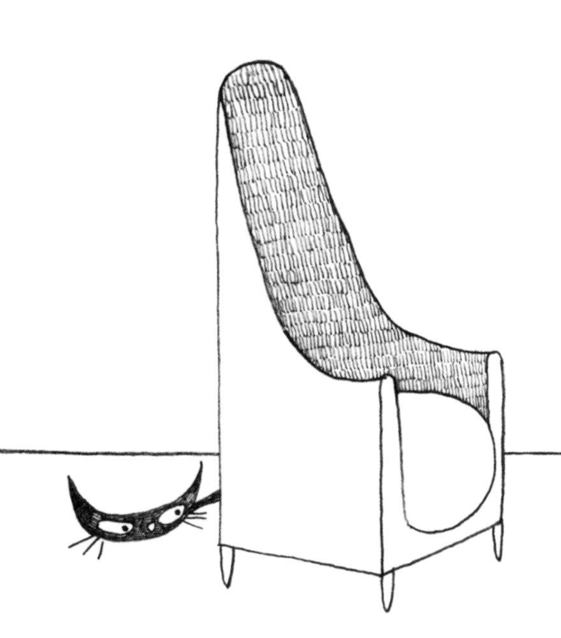

You have but to name it, madam.

"Seeing as how I won't be visiting my apple tree again, maybe you'd pick a sweet little apple for me? I sure would welcome one last deary little taste."

So this *fella*, as skinny as he was long, climbed to the top of the tree, where the apples are the reddest and the sweetest ... and began to choose one ...

“To your left, Mr. D.!

Now to your right!

Now a little higher!

Now a little lower! Yep, that's the one!"

But when it came to getting down, Mr. D. found that
HE WAS STUCK FAST!

And he dangled there all that autumn ...

and all of winter ...

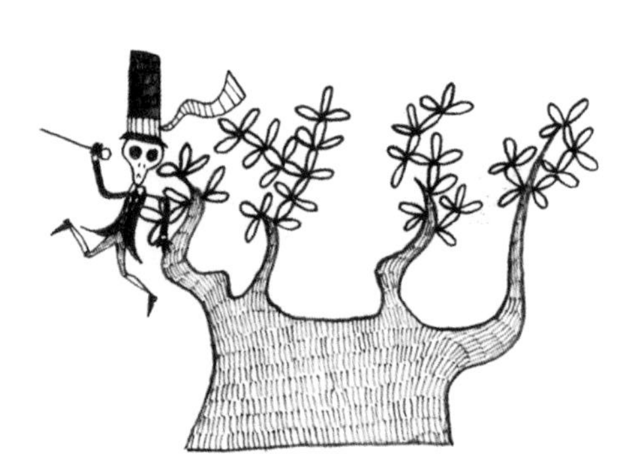

and into spring ...

and well into summer.

And then one day says I to him: "I'll tell you how it's going to be, Mr. D. You can come down if you let me live forever ... yep, FOREVER ... and you can do the same for old Rutterkin here, too."

It was all over for him now, whichever way he wiggled. He had no choice but to grant my wish to live forever ... yep, forever!

But then he gave three snorts, loud enough to make a hog sick, and shouted:

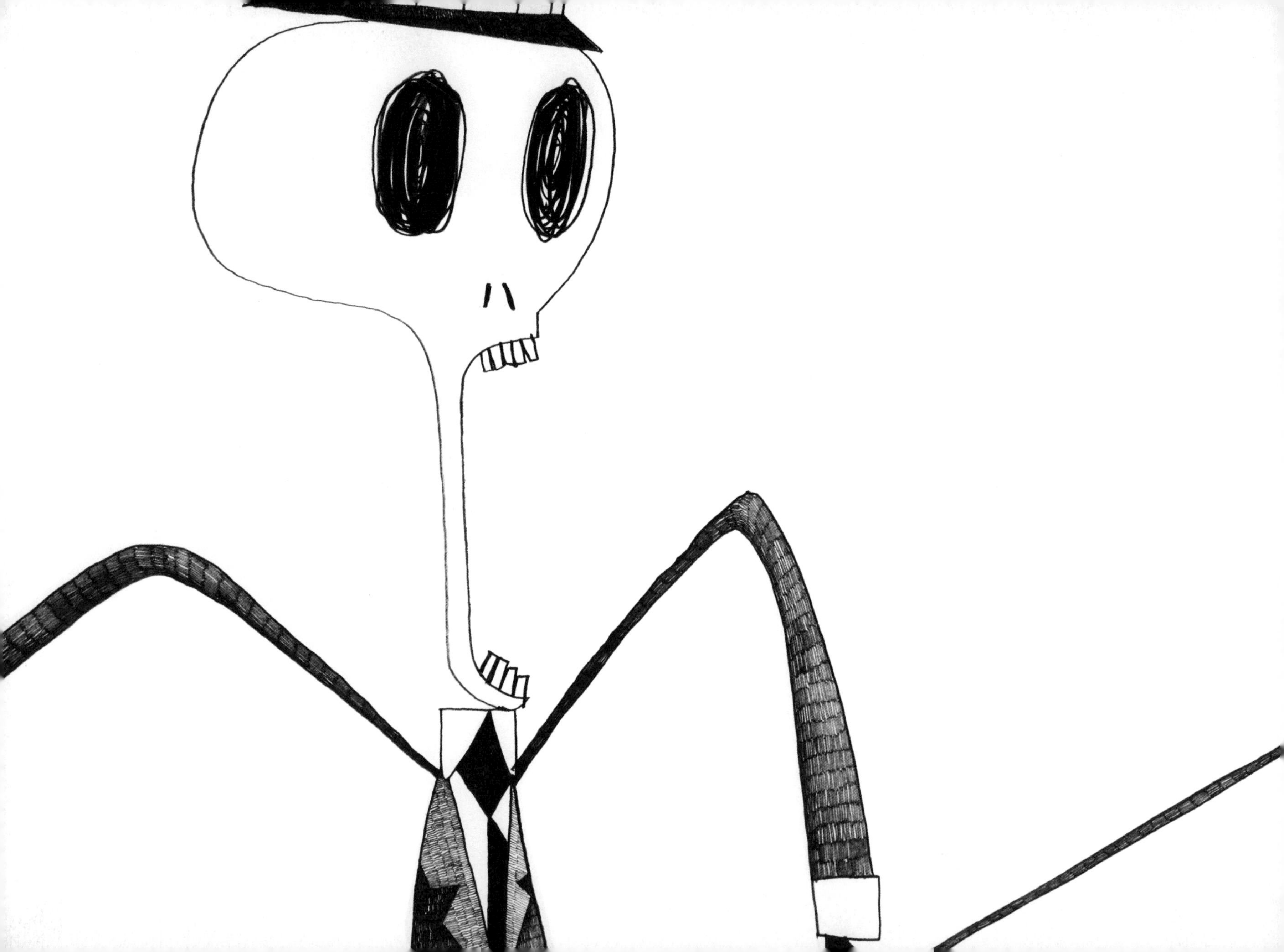

"YOU OLD BEEZUM! MAY YOU HAVE PERPETUAL ITCHING WITHOUT EVER SCRATCHING!"

Well, I'll be jiggered if Mr. D. didn't keep his word. Yep, he did and that!

Isn't that so, Rutterkin, you soft old thing?

Which is why Misery will always be found in this here world ...

... itch, itch, ITCH ...

... itch, itch, ITCH!

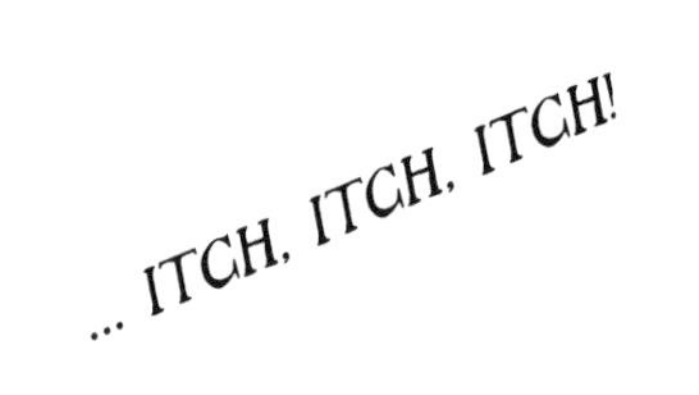

... ITCH, ITCH, ITCH!

... ITCH, ITCH, ITCH!

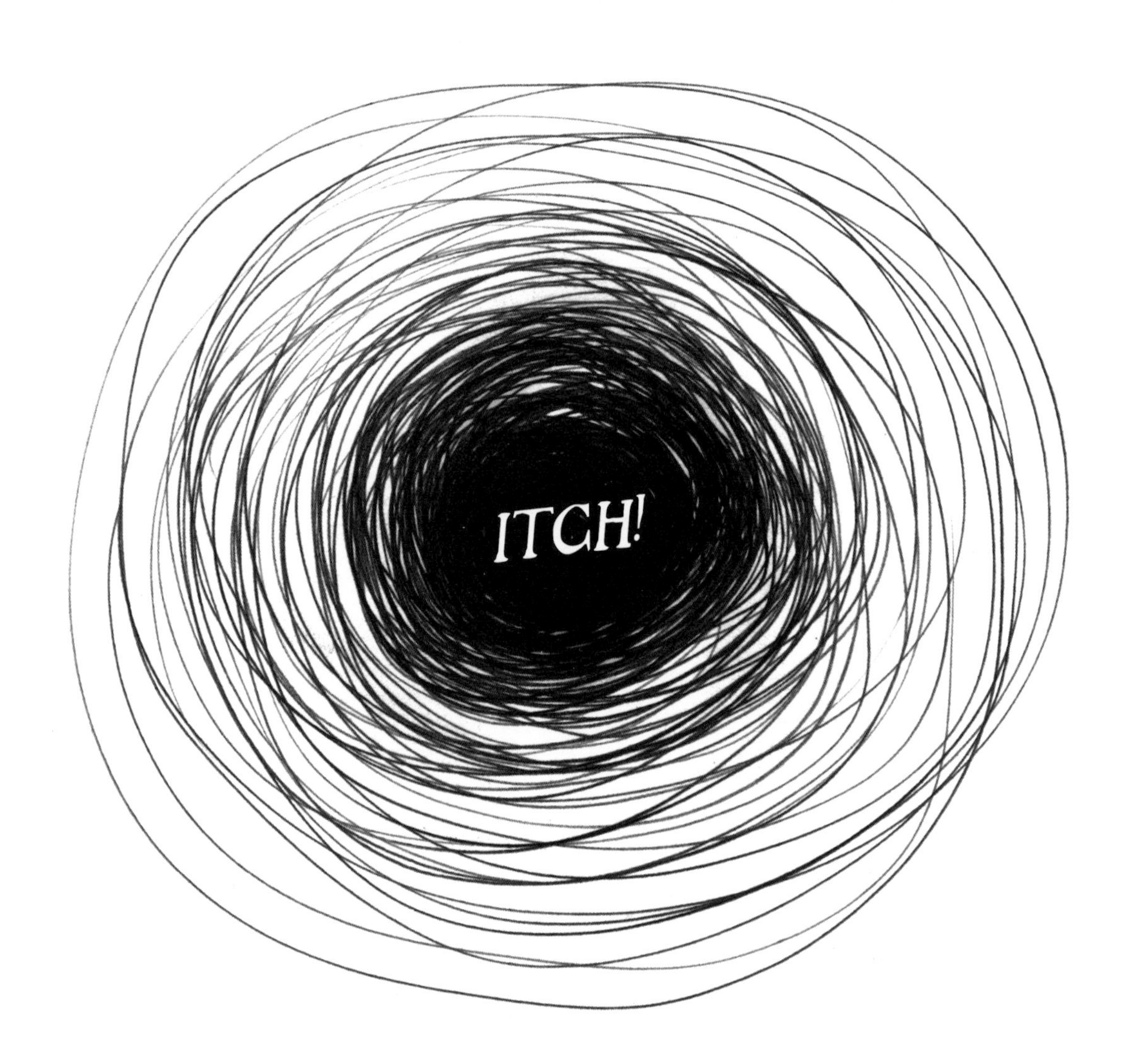
ITCH!